The Coffee Shop, A New Beginning

Athinia Tandino

Published by Athinia Tandino, 2022.

THE COFFEE SHOP, A NEW BEGINNING

First edition. September 19, 2022.

Copyright © 2022 Athinia Tandino.

ISBN: 979-8223021148

Written by Athinia Tandino.

The Coffee Shop:
A New Beginning.

~ Dedicated To Those Left Behind ~

I TELL PEOPLE, "NEVER say Never," because the impossible is only an idea still to do. To try and fail is not the mark of failure. But seeing something as impossible before you have ever tried. It is genuinely marking yourself as a failure.

Courage is not the absence of fear; it makes people ponder what life has to give. What are they supposed to do with what has been granted to them? Nevertheless, I consider what I still need to finish in my life as what still needs doing.

I sit and think about all those dreams I let slip through my fingers.

I dreamed about being a famous writer. How I would build a sanctuary for abused animals, and even how I would one day open a club for men and women to live a life that others would shun.

Although I have done nothing, I still dream of all these things.

I have written and published a few books, yet I have yet to sell anything. So here I sit, thinking about my life.

This story is about a person's abuse, neglect, and survival, and what they had to endure and cope with throughout the years when they should have been loved but were not.

I am writing this book for those who were not and may not be as fortunate as I was.

Therefore, I dedicate this book to them and my brothers and sisters, who still suffer abuse in their adult lives. I write it for those who cannot seem to break the cycle.

I hope this book will help others understand what happens to the less fortunate in our society, even though you may find yourself sad and in awe as you read my book.

All too often, people are not as fortunate and will not live through the horrors and trials that life will set before them, leaving their stories unheard.

Therefore, I write this story in their honor.

Many times in my young life, the hard times seemed impossible. Nevertheless, with the help of some, I would have called friends before they, too, showed their true colors.

However, with good old-fashion hard work, a little imagination, and ingenuity, things that may have been impossible are often possible, and with the strength to do what is necessary despite their fear.

~ The Beginning. ~

IT IS LATE SEPTEMBER, and I am sitting at my computer, trying to clear my head and write my next novel. It is now after seven in the morning, the only time I have to myself.

I have someone here, but I wish I were on a mountain with a lake or an alcove with mountains behind and the ocean in front.

Sometimes I dream of the little alcove with its cottage loft nestled in the trees.

The cottage is an open floor plan with a garden bathroom.

I am dying just like everyone else, if not from a disease, an accident, or old age.

However, we all wish we could live forever, yet we all know there is no way any of us will.

Me, I was ill-fated from the day I was born.

I should have died that day, but for some reason, the Gods and Goddesses saw fit to pity me and keep me alive.

Only they know why.

All I know is I am sentenced to hell.

Anyways, with my father who loved to claim me as his due and a mother who thought I was evil because I just stared at her for some unknown reason.

For her, I would do nothing but cry or stare.

I wonder what she would think if looking back and seeing what was the matter with her child, she knew that all the crying and staring I had done was because I feared what was done due to the trauma of being molested at such a young age.

It makes you think, doesn't it?

This may not be my best novel, but it is a tale nonetheless.

It makes life seem more accessible, at least for me.

With my ability to escape into the writings of others, my writings may help someone else find an escape of their own.

I dedicate it to all those who are like me and feel their world does not match who they are.

I do not know when my life started. I do know that it was not in my formative years. Nor was it the day my mother gave birth to me.

Some say life is simple, just live it. Others say life is hard.

You must keep your boss happy with your work to avoid getting fired.

You must keep your family happy, show unconditional love and respect, and your siblings to please, or you get the pain they can deal out.

What if you cannot keep your boss happy? Or your family shows you no respect or love, and your siblings just hate you for one of your parents leaving, and they say it is your fault?

You see, I am that sibling that a parent was caught harming, and my mother sent the man she thought loved her away for what she caught him doing to me.

Now you see, I have six siblings that blame me for him having to leave because he was caught harming me at the tender age of six.

He was doing things a father should never do to a child.

I can only remember small things about my father and his so-called love for me.

I remember when my mom would go to work, and he would send my siblings out to get ice cream and play, and I could not go with them.

My father had other plans for me, and it was not that of a child but a woman. I do not think I ever got to be a child, even when I lived in foster care.

From age eight until I was twelve, I lived with a family that was supposed to care for the children they agreed to take in. However, they did not care for us but used us as paid labor.

We never get paid unless you consider the food they fed us and the used or donated clothing they put on our backs and sent to school as payment.

When we got home from school, we had, as they called it, chores.

We had to do our homework and then go out and pull the weeds in their garden, which was about two city blocks long and wide.

We had to tend to the chickens, feed the pigs, do the laundry, and clean the house before dinner was on the table.

If this was not done by the time dinner was on the table, you did not get to eat that night.

For four years, I thought this was how life was supposed to be.

I would watch how other children's parents treated their kids while I waited to board the school bus that took us to school or brought us back to the foster home.

I always wondered why those parents gave their children hugs and kisses or met them at the bus stop; I never received that. I would watch the foster mother hug my sisters and brother.

I watched them all.

I was called the water of life when I was young, and I wondered why I was always left out of that tiny bit of affection.

Later in life, I discovered what it meant to be the water of life. I was only born to be used for cleaning like water would do to the day it rained outside.

When one of my siblings did something wrong, and the foster parents did not know who did it, we would have to choose a marble out of a hat, and the one that got the black marble was the one that got the punishment.

I remember the first time I had to get the belt from my foster parent's bedroom and bring it to the foster mother. The first time I got a whipping, I did not know what I had done wrong or why I was being punished.

The foster parent always told us to think about what we had done and why we were getting a whipping.

I had never realized why I was always whipped with a belt until I watched her line us up one day.

My brother was at the head of the line, and I was at the end. And I saw what she was doing with the black marble.

She would hold it in her hand, and when my siblings had taken their white marble, she would drop the black one into the hat, and I knew I would get a whipping.

My sister Tellicia told me one day why I was being whipped. She said she had heard the foster mother tell her husband I was a demonic child, and I needed the devil beat out of me.

On Sundays, we would go to church and tell the pastor, our foster father, about our sins. I did not know what a sin was, and I told the pastor this, and that day when we arrived back at their home, I had to go get the belt and hand it to the foster father this time.

He whipped me so hard that I received minor cuts inside the welts. I was sent to bed without food that day as well.

For four years, I never understood what I had done to be treated by my father as a woman or by the foster parent's whippings post.

I would get up and change the sheets on the bed I slept in because I would wet the bed from the bad dreams of the whippings and my father coming back to harm me sexually.

When I returned to the foster home, I would put the sheets in the washer to do the laundry, and the foster parents would never know I had wet the bed.

Yet they knew. When I got home, they would line us up again, with me at the end and asking who had wet the bed. Not one of my siblings confessed to it but would point at me.

Again, I would have to go get the belt, and once again, I would be whipped and sent to bed without food. I was lucky to eat in the mornings while at school, but I did not get to have dinner for a long time.

It wasn't until I got sick that they started making sure I was given a sandwich for my dinner while my siblings got to eat grand meals.

One day at school, I tried to talk to my teacher about what I had observed; however, she would not listen. She told me to go play, and when I did not, she spit on me and walked away. That is the day I hid in a corner of the playground that no one went to and the day I was forgotten.

I had spent the night in that corner alone, cold, and hungry. I did not know why no one wanted a toe-headed child with light blue eyes so small that everyone overlooked her.

When morning came, I went into the school when the doors opened and to the cafeteria to get something to eat. Still, the cafeteria was empty, and the light was out, and I knew I would have to wait until lunch to eat.

When the children arrived, my brother found me in the library. He told me that I was in trouble for not going home to the foster parents and that they would be picking us up today. I was so scared that I wanted to hide in my corner on the playground. I knew I could not do that because they would find me and know my secret place away from the world of hate.

I went through the day scared of what would happen when I went home with the foster parents. I had not realized that time had gone by fast, and I had not eaten that day.

The foster parents showed up and came and got me from my classroom. The foster mother was not happy to see me either. When she grabbed my little hand and calmly walked me out of the school, I made no sound about her squeezing my hand so hard it hurt.

I knew if I made a sound, I would get punished. I was taught that the punishment would worsen if you made a sound. When she brought me back to her home and had me get the belt, she could not whip me for the cuts, and the welts were too severe and had not healed from the last time her husband had punished me.

My back, butt, and legs still hurt from the whipping I had received the day before. Sitting in the chair at school hurt, but no one seemed to notice or care that I had been abused by people who were supposed to care for me. Yet no one cared about a tiny child like me.

The days passed, and the marks healed, yet it never lasted long. I received a beating again; however, this time, it was for something my brother did and the day I hid in my secret corner.

I had been in the field pulling weeds; my brother was supposed to get a chicken for dinner that night; however, he did not feel like it and told me to get the chicken; although I was doing what I was told to, I still received a whipping for not getting the chicken or finishing pulling the weeds.

Again, we were lined up, and this time I opened my mouth and said something about the marble being an unfair system. I was always getting the whippings, and no one seemed to care about a tiny young girl like me.

The foster mother told me if I was as beautiful as my sisters or functional like my brother and not a child that would disobey a father that was only trying to show me love, I would be in the God's and Goddesses' grace and not have to be punished for the devil's work I had done to tear a family apart as I had done.

This is the punishment Gods and Goddesses had set forth, and it is the punishment one such as I will receive until the Gods and Goddesses see fit to release me.

One day we were called to the living room, and I feared it was for another whipping. However, it was for the faster parents to inform us that we would visit our grandmother that coming Saturday.

I was excited that I would be getting to go as well. I could not wait to go see a grandmother I had never met.

It was a way for me to ask someone if what was happening to us was the way the world or if how I saw my classmates' parents treated their children was how a natural parent treated them. However, my hopes were dashed when the foster mother told me I could not accompany the others to meet our grandmother.

My foster mother told me she did not want to meet the devil child who killed her twin in the womb. I was not worth being around, and they could do what they wanted to the piece of shit that was birth from her child who had sinned.

All I could think of was that the person they were talking about was my mother, and I felt sorry for the woman they were speaking of. Her mother seemed to be treating her as I had been treated, and I began to understand what my mother had gone through with her own.

I remember one day, she came home from asking my grandmother for help. My mother had been severely beaten while pregnant with my baby sister Monkica, which is why we wound up in foster care.

I remember stories of when my sister Tellicia was born. She was born green, somewhat like a lima bean, with a full head of red hair.

I remember being told the stories of my father stating that she was no child of his because of how she looked and how my older brother was not even worth his time since he could not give him what he needed. My mother thought he would be happy because she had given him a son first, but my father was not.

I remember my mother crying a lot and telling her friend about what my father would say and call her how she was so drawn that she did not have the love to give to her children.

I do not really remember my father since he was gone a lot because he was in the military. When he came home from his deployments, I was scared to see the man I remember harming me and would try to hide. However, he would always find me and take what he called his rightful due.

I am older now, and my memories are not what they should be. That is only because of the one day I did get to meet the grandmother, who thought she would be rid of a demonic child by hitting me in the head with a ball ping hammer.

My brother Miguel told me our grandmother told the paramedics I had fallen and hit my head on the edge of the hardwood coffee table.

Miguel told me they believed her, and when the foster parents showed up at the hospital, he told them what happened.

Once we were all in the car and on the way back to the foster care parent's home, I knew I would be punished for what the doctors saw on my body.

Miguel told me the following day that the foster parents told the doctors that my grandmother must have done the damage while I was visiting her.

I knew then that my life would be nothing more than abuse and that I would have to find a way to break the cycle one day.

I also knew I could never be a mother to ensure I did not pass on my horrid life to an innocent.

I have lived my life wondering if this was all I was worth or if there was something better out there. So here I sit still, trying to find the peace I seek and the freedom I urn for.

So here is a story to help those find their peace and freedom.

~ The Coffee Shop A New Beginning ~

IT IS A SWEET SEMI-warm September morning. I could not sleep, so I decided to make my coffee early, sit on the wrap-around porch, and think of my next move.

I know I have to escape the life I am trapped in with a man who thinks I am his property and is too dumb to think for myself.

Some say words do not hurt, and others say they hurt worse than being hit by a giant fist.

Well, I am here to tell you that they hurt more than being hit by a ham-handed fist.

I have had both thrown at me by one person or another, sometimes simultaneously.

I have been beaten so severely because of who and what I am; I found myself in the hospital and the mental ward for the abuse I had sustained.

Being a woman gives men the right to tell you what a piece of shit we all are. Men can use us however they want, for we are nothing but the thing to torcher and torment in one form or another.

Yes, we are women. Women should be respected. But let me tell you, you are mistaken if you think you have fought your way out of the nineteen twenties to be appreciated by any man.

Ever since I was born, I have been told that I am nothing but a piece of shit and should have died or drowned at birth, that I am nothing but the shit on a man's shoes that needs to be scraped off.

If I cry or my feelings get hurt, I need to suck it up, or my favorite is to pull up my bootstraps and deal with it.

At one point, I could no longer pull up my bootstraps or suck it up.

I would rather be alone than walk on eggshells to please a man.

The beating I took last night was one of the worst, but I survived it as I did the rest; if I do not abscond soon, I know the subsequent beating, I will not wake up.

I have been hiding every bit of money I can get my hands on.

Nevertheless, how can I flee the man who will never let me go?

We are not rich, and there is nothing I can sell, get any more money to squander away, and I do not wish to keep selling myself.

He has done enough of that. So, I will ask him if I can get a job close to home to help out more then I do not have to sell myself at night as he requested; maybe he will allow me to get a job at one of the restaurants.

If he will, I can see if the boss will help me open a bank account and put half my pay and the other half in a check to take home to the husband.

I should never have married. When I have enough money to run as far as possible, I will have to find someone to help me with a fake ID and other things I know I will need, yet I know he will not stop looking for me because I am his only meal ticket.

He is too lazy to get a real job, and beating women makes him too happy to do anything else.

He agreed I could work and bring home some cash for his needs. So, I have saved and hope it is enough to escape.

It is now late October, and fifteen years after I got my first job, I have saved enough to make my flee, and now I can abscond the man who said he would never let me go.

When he finds out that I have taken all his money to be able to buy the things I will need and the two hundred and forty-two thousand I stole from him and saved is going to get me killed if I do not go now. I know he will find and kill me for it.

The night air is much too cold for this time of year, and I thought I would never make it down the mountain in my worn second-hand coat.

I had been planning to abscond for three years now. I had saved up the money to buy a small cottage in Dolan, Scotland. I sent the money to the realtor for the little log cabin advertised in the magazine I read at the restaurant where I worked and fell in love with it.

I had everything set. A car was hidden on the main street of the small town of Aspen, Colorado. New identity cards, prepaid credit cards, and enough money to make it until I could stand on my own two feet again.

However, I had planned my route poorly. The trees and bushes had come out in the night like little demons clawing at my skin as if trying to stop me from leaving the nightmare I had been living.

The city's lights came into view; although I knew I was not home free, I still had to sneak through the town and make it safely to my car without being seen by my husband's family and friends.

As I rounded the corner, I saw my husband's sister Charlotte standing at the door of Cantina's restaurant. Where my husband, Lawrence, and Charlotte, his sister, were to meet for the Halloween dinner being held for his company.

I waited until I felt the coast was clear, so I could hurry down the street to where my car was waiting.

I knew I had to make it without drawing attention to myself.

Finally, they all had gone in, and the way was evident when I spotted someone standing by my car. I did not know what to do, so I walked into the nearest open store and watched as the man left my car just as I had left it.

Hurrying towards my car, I dug into my pocket for the keys, rushing to open the door, when I saw the man by my car turning the corner.

Finally, the door opened, and I climbed in as fast as possible and locked the doors as I started the engine.

When I saw two more men turn the corner just behind the first, as I slowly pulled out onto the street, I thought, 'I am finally free.' Now all I had to do was drive to the Denver international airport.

I felt relief as if my life was my own again. I did not have to answer anyone.

My mother and father had passed away two years previous in a car accident that could not be explained.

I felt that my husband had something to do with it; however, I had no proof, yet something inside told me he had done it to make sure I depended solely on him.

I had taken classes to help me become dependent on no one but myself; however, I still felt lost and alone. How do these women nowadays do it?

So, I thought as I drove down the long dark highway that seemed to go on forever.

I tried to put the thought out of my mind by turning on the radio. However, that was the one thing in the car I did not check to make sure it worked. So, the silence and the thoughts ran through me, almost as if someone had opened the floodgates.

I decided that these thoughts would keep me from leaving and drive me back to the life I was escaping.

Trying hard not to think about how things were, I decided to put my mind to what was yet to come.

This gave me the strength to move forward with the new life I wanted.

I started thinking about everything I wanted to do with my life. How could I write or even have a Coffee Shop where people could relax and read?

I thought about how to start painting again as I did before I married Lawrence, who made me feel as if I was worthless and no good at anything. However, I knew I was good at painting and writing; I would do this again without harm when I tried to have something of my own. This kept me going.

I saw the sign that pointed me to freedom: five miles ahead. I would be at the airport in no time, and before my husband and his sister returned to the house on the mountain, I would be on the plane and in the air when they found me gone.

I told my husband I was too ill to attend the Halloween party, so he allowed me to stay home. But promise me that I will pay for not attending his company's party. He said this was his new job, and I was disrespecting him by not going. So, I had better prepare myself for my punishment.

When I saw his car disappear down the driveway, I dressed in the second-hand clothes I had bought two weeks before. Hiding them in the pantry behind the sack of potatoes where I knew he would never look.

Now it was confirmed with the airport lights just in front of me. As I drove into the free parking lot, I knew this would be the last time I would see my car, but that no longer mattered to me, for just a few feet ahead were the doors that would take me to my new life.

Getting the rest of the things I had bought from the trunk of the car and the new identification, I headed for the double doors that would lead me to freedom. As I entered the building, I knew I would not have to wait in a long line since I had nothing to check in. All I owned could be carried in the gym bag and the small backpack purse. In addition, I knew I could obtain more clothing when I arrived.

I headed for the e-ticket booth to retrieve my tickets to Arran Scotland. I would have to find a way to Dolan from there, but I will worry about that when the time comes.

It was almost two when I boarded the plane and sat in the center aisle. I was scared but relieved to be on the way to a new life.

Nervousness and excitement washed over me all at once; I had no friends and did not know anyone there, but I felt the new life I could make there would have them in no time.

I was sitting there thinking about the name I had chosen for myself. I am Milly Windalmire; I knew I would have to get used to being called by my new name so that no one suspected this was not who I am.

'I am Milly Windalmire; I repeatedly said in my mind until I was comfortable with the new name when I felt the plane start to move.

'I am a good person, kind, loving, caring,' I thought about who I am and how I wanted others to see me.

Then, I felt the plane slowly lifting into the air, and I thought about who I was before I married.

'Should I be the person I was before I got married? On the other hand, I could be the person I have always wanted to be. Who am I?

My thoughts had drawn me deep inside myself. I was trying to figure out who I was when I felt a hand on my shoulder that brought my fears to the surface.

As I slowly looked up, I saw a sweet smile on the flight attendant's face.

"Do you need anything, hun?" the attendant asked as I tried to bring my fears under control.

"No, thank you," I said calmly.

"If you need anything, call me. I am Maya," the attendant said as she slowly walked away, leaving me to my thoughts again.

As I sat there deep in thought, with the roaring of the engines and the desperate need to be free drowning out the world around me, I could not help but wonder if I could make it on my own.

The thought of my new name being played repeatedly made it easier to use it freely now. That is who I am and who I wish to be.

The flight will stop in Newark, New Jersey, with an hour-and-a-half layover. So, I will have been gone from Colorado for almost four hours.

After the layover, I will be back on the flight. Finally, to freedom, for almost seven hours, I have been looking for. I will arrive in Glasgow, Scotland, then take the train to Arran. It will take another six hours and then a cab to Dolan, where I will catch the ferry across the waters to my new home.

I sat there thinking about all the traveling I would have to do. I finally feel safe and accessible.

Even though I had to fly to get to the point I wanted to be, I can feel deep down that it was all worth it. I will never have to leave the safety of my new home.

There are only two ways onto Arran Island, one is by train, and the other is by ferry, where you can only bring your car with permission from the government.

I knew then that I would know long before anyone came that I was being looked for; this would give me enough time to escape deep into the woods if needed.

I decided to buy myself a bike so that I would be able to get around. Of course, I would have to have the things I purchased delivered, but that was okay with me, too, for I would be safe in my home, hidden away from all.

I knew that when I rode around, I would get to know the natives of the island and be able to become friends with them.

This made me smile since it would be the first time I could have my own friends in many years.

I thought about the cottage and how it looked in the brochure. The furniture looked antique, but it was mostly wood but old.

The cottage had not been lived in for about four years, and I knew I would have to stop and pick up some things I would need to put the cottage back in order.

"Return your seats to their upright positions," I heard the captain say as they descended.

~ The Airport ~

"WE WILL BE ARRIVING at Newark International terminal in about five minutes," he said as I felt the wheels bump against the pavement as they touched the ground.

As the plane stopped, I started feeling anxious; slowly, I got to my feet, retrieved my bag from the overhead, and made my way to the terminal. I decided to stay in the airport until it was time to return to the plane again.

Set in mind what I had to do when I arrived in Dolan, I started making a list of all the things I would need. I hoped a store would be open so I could acquire everything I needed to clean my new home.

Sitting in the area where I was to catch my next flight, I could not help but feel as if someone was watching me; slowly, I turned to see a redheaded little boy looking at me.

Smiling, I returned to finish my list of everything I needed. The list had everything from linens for the bed, food to get me by for a few days, to cleaning supplies I would need to bring the cottage back to life.

The time seemed to fly by, for the next thing I heard was the person at the counter coming over to the loudspeaker, stating that they would be boarding soon.

Putting my notepad back in my purse, I gathered my bag and headed for the line in front of the terminal gate. As I made my way down the duct and onto the plane to find my seat, I saw the same flight attendant that had traveled with me from Colorado.

Maya smiled, took my bag from me again, and placed it in the overhead compartment as I had before. I still felt uncomfortable with my things being touched by a stranger.

Still, I knew it was my job when I saw myself do the same for the woman and little redheaded boy behind me, which set me at ease.

As the plane filled with passengers, I knew I would be safe and halfway to my new life when I landed in Glasgow.

All I would need to do then was catch the train to Arran and then a cab to a store to gather the things I would need for a few weeks. Then I hoped that the cabs would be able to take me the rest of the way to my new home.

Sitting back and listening to the flight attendants as they went through their customary ritual on the safety rules. I could not help but notice that Maya had been watching me.

I watched Maya disappear behind the curtain when the announcement was over.

Then the plane started moving again. I knew I would never have to worry again; I would be in a land where no one knew my background or the life I had to live.

Although something made me keep my guard up, even though I did not know what or who it was, I felt I would never be able to let it down. Maybe one day, I could relax and open up to a relationship or friend; however, I would not let anyone in for now.

I had my life now and would make it what I wanted, not what I was told and forced.

Feeling more at ease, I laid back to try and get some sleep. However, the excitement of a new start in life made me unable to, so I started to daydream about how I wanted my life to be and everything I would do.

I would have breakfast on the beach, then put in a small garden of vegetables, and maybe I would put flowerbeds in the front by the stairs to the deck that led to the front door.

I thought about how I would make the antique furniture look new again and how the cottage would look from the photographs in the brochure.

The main floor was wide open, with nothing to separate the living room area from the kitchen and dining room. However, it has big bay windows so I could see the area around my home from anywhere I stood, making it bright and comfortable.

Under the loft was the bathroom almost as big as the bedroom I had shared with Lawrence. It has a sunken garden tub that sits caddie corner, with a bay window where I can put plants that would scent the room with their beautiful aroma. So, I could relax when I took my nightly bath. The double black sink and toilet surrounded by linen cabinets of oak made me smile.

Sleep must have come to me, for the captain's voice awakened me over the loudspeaker that jolted me out of what seemed to be a fabulous dream.

"We will arrive at the Arran International Airport in about ten minutes. Please put your seats back into their upright position; the seat belt sign is now on," he said with a strange accent that made me giggle.

As the plane's wheels touched the ground, something inside me came to life. The sense of being free overwhelmed me, and the tears began to stream down my face; wiping them away so no one saw; I noticed that Maya had been watching the whole time.

"Are you all right?" Maya asked in a whisper and with a great deal of concern.

"Yes, thank you, I am fine. I am just happy to be landing," I said as I tried to read Maya's face to see if I had bought the lie I had just told.

"Miss, Can we talk when I get off work?" Maya said as I watched. I quickly gathered my things to escape as soon as they landed; however, Maya would not let me move until I had answered.

"All right," I said, then turned to get my purse from the empty seat next to me.

Maya knew this young woman would bolt like a scared rabbit if she were out of sight.

Turning, she whispered to her co-worker, and the next thing I knew, I was being watched as Maya went behind the curtain and returned with her bags.

Maya made her way to my side, leaving the plane together. I could not help but feel out of place as we walked silently into the airport.

Once we were out the front doors of the airport terminal, Maya turned to me.

"I know you are running from something; however, I do not know what just yet. Please do not be scared; it is easier said than done. I want you to know I will not let any harm come to you," Maya said as a small smile came over her face,

Maya hoped this would put me at more ease.

"What makes you think I am running from something?" I said as I watched the smile on Maya's face fade.

"I was once in your place. Come, we will take my car, and I will take you wherever you are going," Maya said as she led me to a small silver Matai.

After securely packing all the bags in the trunk of Maya's car, I climbed into the passenger seat. I sat quietly until Maya started moving towards what looked to be the highway.

"How were you once in the place you say I am in?" I tried to ask with a calm voice.

"The man I was with about eight years ago tied to kill me. He is now dead, executed by the state; however, I still do not feel safe, even though his family is far away and harbors no ill will towards me, and his face still haunts me. I still feel as if my life is not my own. I guess that is how I can see that you are from some nightmarish life. You came here to hide. You are alone and unsure of how you will make it or if he will show up again one day and try to make you return to that life. So that you know the people here will welcome you as if you are part of their family. So here is a fair warning, if you are asked who you are, make sure you are ready to tell them. You probably have changed your name and made sure you have enough money

to make it if you manage it wisely. Have you acquired a place to live?" Maya asked with the most sympathetic look on her face.

"Yes, I own my place in Dolan. It took me a while to come up with the money, but yes, I have a place to live. Why do you ask?" I asked as I watched the surprised look come over Maya's face.

"Most women I know who have tried to escape an abusive relationship do not think that far ahead. Some say they will acquire something when they find a safe enough place. Others find that it is too hard and go back. I am glad you thought about that before you ran," Maya said as she glanced at me.

"Why are you telling me this?" I asked as I turned to watch the scenery out the side window.

"I know how it was when I left my husband. I can see how you are feeling and how scared you are; however, you do not need to fear anything anymore because you now have a friend that understands what you are going through. What is your name now? Not the name you once had but the name you have chosen for yourself. The one you want everyone to know you as," Maya asked with a crooked smile laid upon her face.

"Milly... Milly Windalmire is the name I found on the internet that made me feel like who I was before I got married," I told her as I stared at the sun starting to rise.

"So, where do you live?" I asked as I watched the world outside the car window go by like a daydream.

"Well, you will be surprised. I live on the island of Dolan. We will have to take the ferry over," Maya told me as I sighed.

"Oh... so you can take your car onto the island?" I asked in surprise.

"Yes... I have lived on the island for almost three years now. I had to wait for two of those to get the right to have a car so that I could come and go as I please," Maya said as I giggled at the fact that my new friend knew about the island's laws.

"How do you know so much about the island life here?" Maya asked, hoping it would break the silence I could feel was coming.

"*I researched my heritage while looking for a place to hide. Then, in college, I always dreamed of coming to Scotland. You know it is funny that my husband never asked what my dreams were, now that I think about it,*" *I said as a smile and a giggle hit my lips.*

I felt my cheeks redden when I saw Maya's face light up at the thought of me giggling without the fear Maya had first seen.

~ The Restaurant ~

"ARE YOU HUNGRY?" MAYA asked as she turned into a quaint-looking diner.

"Yes, a bit," I said, taking in more of the diner's structure.

"Come, I will buy us some breakfast. Then, we can watch the sun as it comes up out of the ocean just behind the restaurant," Maya said as we got out of the car and she pushed the button to lock the doors.

I followed Maya to the restaurant in silence. The server was waiting to seat us as we walked through the front door.

"We would like a place on the deck to watch the sun finish coming up. Is that all right?" Maya asked the server as she led us to a quaint table from the sliding glass doors to the deck hanging over the ocean.

"Will this table do, ladies?" she asked, then saw me walking towards a table by the railing.

"What may I get you two lovely ladies to drink?" she asked. As she watched us take our seats.

Maya looked over at me. "Is coffee okay?" she asked as I sat across from my new friend and saw me nod approvingly.

"Aw... Perfect spot for a new beginning," Maya said as she watched me looking down at the water as it made its way to shore and back out again.

"You seem confused or as if something is wrong, Milly," Maya said as she watched my face pale.

"I do not know if I have done the right thing. I had a good life before I got married. My mother and father were alive then, and we were happy

until he came into our lives. Now they are gone, and I have to leave my home, where I can no longer see them. I wish I knew what to do. I just wanted to be as happy as they had been. Am I doing the right thing, Maya?" I asked with tears in my eyes.

Maya handed me a napkin to dry the tears. While she searched her heart for the words that would bring her friend some comfort; however, she could not find the words that would not seem false, so she decided that the truth may hurt. Still, it was the best thing for her to hear right now.

"Hun... You will one day find you have, by leaving the man who tried to harm you, even may have killed you if you had not left him. Now you can have a happy life without ties to bind you anywhere. You are now free to live your life without fear. Now sweety, all you have to do is accept it. I would love to have what you have now; I live in a small cottage. So, you have a home to start your life. You have planned it all out. I bet you even have a list of what you want to get and do down to the last detail. How you want your home to look, maybe even have a garden, a couple of flower gardens; I bet you even live on the beach so you can have your morning coffee as you watch the sun come out of the ocean. I will go as far as betting you have a list in your bag on the things you will need to buy to clear, maybe a grocery list, so you do not go hungry," Maya said as she took a sip of her coffee.

"You know, Milly, when I came here, I had nothing. I worked all the time trying to save money to buy this special cottage in Dolan. When I saw it for the first time, I found a sold sign, which was the day my heart sank. I asked the real-estate person who had bought it; however, she refused to tell me and said something about a privacy act. So, I have been sitting here wondering. Are you the one that bought Mr. and Mrs. Winters house?" Maya asked as she pulled out a brochure identical to the one I had in my bag. The flyer for the small cottage I bought a year ago.

"So that is why you singled me out... you are looking for the person that bought something you wanted and had been saving for; yes, that is my place now. Yes, I have a list of everything I am going to do. I am going to make my life in that cottage. Please do not get up, and thank you for the coffee and

ride this far. However, this is where I will take my leave of you, so please let me live my life in peace," I said as I got to my feet and headed for the door when I remembered that Maya had placed my things in the trunk of her car. Turning around, I saw Maya right behind me.

"I guess you forgot that I had placed your things in the trunk of my car. Please, Milly, come back and have your breakfast and let us talk," Maya said as she took me by the arm and hoped I would not cause a scene.

I went with Maya back to the table peacefully. However, I knew that I would have to go with this woman so that I would be able to retrieve my things.

"I did not mean to upset you. I was not sure if you were the one that had acquired Mr. and Mrs. Winters cottage or not. I am glad it went to someone that could use a new start in life. I am truly sorry for my actions; can you forgive me?" Maya asked.

"I am sorry I took the place you wanted. The day I saw it, I fell in love with it. It took me three years to save every penny I could find. I even took my husband's five hundred dollars a week until I finally came up with the down payment. It took me two years to pay the five hundred every week. I stole five hundred from my husband and took the same from my paycheck to pay it off. I finally got it paid for; ten months ahead of time; I could put the money in prepaid credit cards until they reached their maximum limit; then, I had to open a new one to hide the money. I endured the beatings for not telling him where it all had gone. Therefore, I earned that cottage with my blood and will live there peacefully. Neither you nor anyone else will scare me away from my dream of being free," I said with a scowl.

"I am not going to take you home, Milly. I am truly sorry. I did not know what all you had to go through to get it so that you can be free," Maya said in the most sympathetic voice, and then I saw the waiter coming towards us.

"Looks like it is time for us to order. Do you know what you want? Alternatively, would you like me to order for the both of us?" Maya asked with a faint smile.

"No, thank you, coffee is fine; I am not hungry now, but you go on and eat," I said with a great deal of anger still in my eyes.

"Are you ready to order, or is it just coffee this morning?" the server asked.

"Just coffee... May we get the check, please?" Maya asked as she turned back to me.

"Are you ready to go?" Maya asked me.

"Yes," I said as I watched the waiter walk away, then turned back to Maya.

"I would like my things so I can catch the next train to Arran," I said in a low, gruff voice.

"Milly, please, I will take you to your cottage. We can even gather the things you need to put the cottage back in order if you like. I want to be your friend, and I am truly sorry for what I said and how I acted in the restaurant. Can you please find it in you to forgive me?" Maya pleaded with tears in her eyes.

"You made me relive the life I am trying to escape. You made me feel ashamed of what I did to be able to be free and survive without a man in my life. So now you want me to be your friend? To forgive you for the hate you have shown me when you do not even know who I am," I said.

I realized that Maya sincerely apologized, and the shame washed over me again. I saw in myself that I was acting like those people I hated. The unforgiving, with no compassion for others' feelings, the tears welled in my eyes, and I turned towards the water.

"I am sorry; I should have been more understanding that you also love the cottage, and it was a place of a new beginning as well. I just got it before you; if it were the other way around, I would feel the same way. Can we start over?" I turned and asked Maya.

Maya let out a small giggle through the sobs, "Yes. Hi, I am Maya Tesolini; I see you are new in town; think we could be friends?" Maya said as I dried my tears with a slight giggle.

"Nice to meet you, Maya; I am Milly Windalmire. Yes, I am new in town, and it would be nice to have a friend," I said.

"So, Milly, are you ready to go shopping? I know this great place where you can get everything you need to start a new life here in Scotland. It has cleaning supplies, clothing, and food. Oh, wait, you might know it as Super Wal-Mart's," Maya said as she unlocked the door to her car.

Maya and I started laughing. Finally, we became friends after our rocky start. They felt that they had always been free and friends for a long time. I knew then that I would be all right, and my life was now my own, and I felt I could now get on with my life and forget about the past as if it had never happened.

~ The Shopping Spree ~

AS MAYA AND I DROVE down the highway, Maya pointed out the best places they could go dancing or have a great dinner out. If I was not in the mood to leave Dolan Island, Maya said she would show me some of the island pubs that would tell me about some of the island's cultures.

"In time, you will be just like a native of the island," Maya told me as she pulled into the Wal-Mart parking lot.

I dug in my backpack purse to retrieve the list I had made while I waited to board the plane in Newark, then looked up and saw the smile on Maya's face that seemed to reach from ear to ear. I could not help but start laughing at the fact that Maya already knew about my list.

As we exited the car, Maya looked at me with a childish look of mischief. I knew what Maya had in mind; it was almost as if something pushed me, and I started running with Maya hot on my heels. As they reached the doors, they were laughing like two little schoolchildren.

Maya and I grabbed a cart each and started toward the cleaning supplies. Once we had all we felt needed to do the job, we headed towards the paint counter.

I wanted to restore the cottage to the beautiful home it once was, so I picked the paint carefully.

First, for the outside, I got a deep earth brown for the trim and soft creamy sand for the cottage walls.

I decided I would only need one color for the inside since no walls separate the rooms. I had chosen a deep-water wet sand color for the interior, *and once I had finished getting that, I headed to get the rest of the things on my list.*

We had been shopping for about three hours. Maya could see the carts were getting full and wondered if her small Matai could hold everything they had obtained; however, I felt I had only one thing left to get. I also needed a coffee pot and large cups to fill with the cappuccino.

As I headed towards the kitchen aisle for the last things I needed, Maya headed for the checkout line.

Maya wanted something for a housewarming gift but needed to figure out what to get me.

Maya knew I would need everything, so I waited to see what I had not gotten on this shopping spree.

I was returning to the front with my weighted-down cart, where Maya awaited me.

I could see Maya light up and laugh at my difficulty pushing my cart to the checkout counter. Then, Maya started running to give me a hand with the cart after abandoning her over-loaded cart.

Maya could see for the first time how happy I had looked since she had met me. I was all a glow as if my life had taken a significant turn for the first time. Seeing this made Maya ashamed of what I had done in the restaurant.

Maya remembered the day she had finally left her husband and how she needed a friend, how unsafe she felt, how he had found her, and how he could get into her home and hurt her.

Then came to her the perfect gift. She fumbled around in her over-filled purse, looking for her cell phone. When she finally found it, she hurried to dial the number of a friend who was the locksmith and alarm system specialist for Dolan. Maya wanted Milly to feel safe.

"Hello, is Max there?" Maya asked the receptionist.

"Oh, hello, Maya; how was your trip? "He is standing right here; hold on one second, and I will get him for you," she said.

"Good morning, Maya; what can I do for you?" Max asked.

"Hey Max, I have a friend who has bought the old Winters' place, and I was wondering if you would do me a favor?" Maya whispered over the phone.

"You know I will do anything for you, Maya," Max said.

"Well... I want to give my new friend a housewarming gift to make her feel safe living alone, so I was wondering if you have time today. Could you install an alarm that will protect the whole house and property? No matter the cost, I know you will give me a good deal," Maya said.

"Sure, I can come out this afternoon and start putting it in if that will be good for you?" Max said.

"That will be perfect. After that, we will clean up the house and give it a new coat of paint," Maya said.

"Okay, I will be there at noon. See you then." Max said.

"All right, see you then," Maya said as she hung up the phone.

"So, are we almost done? Alternatively, are we missing anything?" Maya asked in a teasing manner.

"No, I think I got everything; I bought out of the store," I laughed.

Maya took one cart while I handled the other. We headed towards the door with the two loaded-down heavy carts when Maya looked over at me with that same childish look in her eyes that I had when we first got there. Seeing the look, I gave my cart one healthy heave and started running the best I could to make it back to Maya's car before she did; however, the carts were too heavy, and the girls had made it there simultaneously. Laughing and hugging each other, they started to load the car with the newly acquired pieces.

After Maya and I loaded the car, Maya stepped back to look at the sight. We had managed to put everything into her tiny car. But, unfortunately, it started to look like U-Haul. So, we started laughing at how the vehicle was overpacked.

We could not close the trunk lid because it housed the gardening plants and herbs for the kitchen windowsill. It was loaded so full that we wondered if any room was left to enter.

"Well, let us get going. If we are going to make it there before noon, we had better leave now," Maya said, laughing as they squeezed into the front seats and headed slowly down the highway toward the ferry.

"So... when we get there, what do you want to do first? "Well, after we unload the car," Maya asked with a smile plastered across her face.

"Well... I want to start cleaning the kitchen, so I can cook dinner and place the herbs on the windowsill to make a warm and inviting place," I said with a concerned look.

I had seen Maya on the phone; however, I could not hear what was being said or whom she was talking to, making me nervous.

"Mind if I help? I am a great cook and can handle a paintbrush," Maya stated.

"I would love the help, although, you know what is said about too many cooks in the kitchen. I will cook for you since you are my guest," I said as I laughed at the thought of being able to kick someone out of the kitchen, my kitchen.

They finally reached the ferry just in time. The ferry hand was about to close the gate when he saw the car approaching him. It looked like it was packed by someone that had gone on a mad shopping spree, and then he recognized the car and started laughing and waving for Maya to stop so that he could bring her car on for her.

Maya laughed because she knew George would never allow her to drive her car onto the ferry again.

She stopped the vehicle atop the ramp. Maya got out and motioned for me to follow.

"Good morning, George, this is Milly Windalmire, she bought the old Winters cottage, and we are going to bring it back to life. So, what have you been doing with yourself?" Maya asked, then winked at me.

"Good morning, Lassies; it is nice to meet you, Miss Milly. I am George Thornguser. It is nice to have you added to our small community. How was your trip, Lass?" George asked, then winked at Maya as he got into the car to bring it aboard the ferry.

"It was good, George. We had a small layover in Newark, but other than that, it was a smooth trip. We are going to get some coffee to keep warm. See you later, George," Maya yelled back in the car's direction as I put my arm in hers and headed for the small café.

"George is a great guy; however, he will never let me bring my car onto the ferry after my small accident the first time I tried," Maya said with a slight giggle.

Maya and I sat in the small room that was supposed to be a Coffee Shop. However, it was just a building with a small table with chairs and a vending machine of sorts, and a coffee pot on a counter.

Even though things were different, I still had this gnawing feeling about Maya. I wanted to know how Maya had known I had changed my name. Something did not feel right, and I did not know if I should ask, but I felt I had to.

"Maya, may I ask you a question?" I said with what little courage I had left.

Fear ran through me, and I did not know if I wanted to know the answer.

"You may ask me anything," Maya said and saw the fear had risen again.

"How did you know I had changed my name? What did I do to give you that impression? Sorry, this is two questions, but I need to know," I whispered as I tried to hide the fear in my voice.

"When we were on the plane, I laid my hand on your shoulder, and you nearly jumped out of your skin. I was not sure if I had just startled you or what. Then I remembered how I felt when I found out that my husband had killed three people, and I ran to hide, how I would jump at every little thing," Maya said as she took a sip of her coffee and looked out the window.

"So, I watched you. You tried to sleep but couldn't; you seemed focused on other things. When we landed in Glasgow, and I had cornered you, you were like a trapped rabbit. That is when I knew you had been abused," Maya said as she looked back to see the fear slowly fading from Milly's eyes.

"When they executed my husband for his crimes, Which was the first time my life felt safe and free. After that, I told you I would never ask you about your past, and I mean it," Maya said as she retrieved another cup of coffee.

"Milly, you are not that person any longer. You are the person I see before me. A kind, caring, yet scared, and I know how you feel and what you are going through. I do not know you yet, but in time we will be like sisters," Maya said as she returned to the small table and placed her hand on mine.

"I told you at the restaurant that I wanted a friend after my nightmare. I needed someone to talk to, to be there when I broke down; however, I never had that. That is when I promised myself that if I ever encountered someone who showed signs of how I once felt, I would try to become friends with them. Let them know they are not alone and that many women have escaped a life of pain, so here we sit, sharing our past or what we want to share. Does this ease your mind?" Maya asked with tears in her eyes and saw the tears rolling down her face and remembered how she had longed to have someone to lean on.

"Oh, Maya, I am so sorry; I did not mean to hurt you. Please forgive me. You are right. I need a friend to help me be the person you have described. You see things in me that I cannot see just yet. Yes, I am hiding from a nightmare of a life, One that I want to forget. I do not know how or whom I can trust. I want to be a good person that is not black and blue. I do not want to hide or pretend I am too sick to see anyone when someone comes to the door because I have been beaten so badly that you cannot make out who I am. I do not want to live in fear any longer," I said as the tears ran down my face like a small stream overflowing.

Maya moved to the chair next to me and slowly placed her arms around me, pulling me close. Maya knew I had not grieved for the person I once was and had killed myself by changing my name. However, Maya knew I did not realize that once my name changed, I was killing the old life to begin a new one, to be free from harm, and to live the way I had always hoped.

Maya knew she needed to be a good friend to this lost soul that lay weeping in her arms; she knew I would need more security to feel safe from the world. She would need someone to lean on for when the times got hard that was still yet to come.

"Let it out, hun; you will feel much better when you have had a good cry," Maya said with so much compassion.

Maya felt me relax, so she slowly moved away, reached into her purse, pulled out a powder blue Kleenex, and handed it to me.

"Now dry your eyes, and let us discuss your new life here. What do you want to do?" Maya asked as she pulled out another Kleenex to dry her own eyes.

I looked up at Maya with a few more sniffles.

"Well, I want a small bookstore and Coffee Shop. A place I can call my own, where people can come and read or bring in their laptops, whatever they want to do. Maybe where they could come to have brunch or lunch, something that represents me," I said with a smile, slowly appearing at the thought of running my own business.

Maya watched my eyes as they lit up at the thought of having a place that was my own, where I could have a friend and live without fear.

"Milly, I know a place where you can make your dreams come true. There is a small store run by an older couple that already had a Coffee Shop and books; however, it is outdated and would need a lot of work. Also, it has a small apartment over the top. I would love to stop traveling and have a life as well. Maybe we can take that over, and I could live there," Maya said with a dreamy look.

~ Cleaning Out the Old ~

"I NEED TO SETTLE IN first and make the cottage my own before I do anything else. I only have sixty thousand dollars left, and I know the cottage will need some to fix it back up. We do not even know if the people want to sell," I said.

"You are right. I will take a few weeks off of work and help you get the cottage in shape; this way, we can get to know each other better. Then, when that is done, we can go and talk to them and see if they want to sell. If they do, I can help with the money to get it started and have an attorney write the papers to make us partners. But, nevertheless, let us concentrate on the cottage first," Maya said with a sparkle in her eyes.

"You do not even know me; why do you want to be a partner with someone you do not even know?" I asked as I watched Maya's eyes come back into focus from her dreamy state.

"I have always wanted to settle down, to have a life where I could one day own my own home and have children. A place I could also call my own. I long to be a mother and raise a little boy and girl, just like the little redheaded boy on the plane," Maya said with tears running down her face.

I sat there watching as Maya dried her eyes; I could not help but feel compassion for my friend's need to start living.

I knew then that I had a friend for the first time since I had been away from my husband; this was something I had not had in a long time.

Lawrence had taken all my friends I had before they got married and made them either disappear or stop being my friend altogether. So, this was the first time I felt I could have something of my own in fifteen years.

As they sat there talking, they heard the door to the small coffee area open and turned to see George walking in. He made his way to the almost empty coffeepot; Maya knew then that they were almost to the dock of Dolan.

"So, George, how far from shore are we?" Maya asked as she got to her feet.

"We have been on shore for about fifteen minutes. I saw you two talking and thought you needed some time. I did not want to interrupt. So, I parked your car in the lot just up the hill and have Sam watching it, so nothing gets taken," George said as he handed Maya the keys, then turned and winked at me as he made his way out the door.

"Well, thank you, George. Shall we get moving," Maya asked me as she sat down what was left of her coffee on the counter and headed for the door.

I said nothing; I just set my coffee on the table and followed Maya. The silence seemed deafening as we traveled off the ferry and up the hill toward Maya's car.

I could not help but wonder what was on Maya's mind. Yet, I could only watch out the window as the scenery passed.

The road curved and wined almost into nowhere when Maya turned right onto a small dirt road that looked like it had been encased in a forest of trees for miles. That was when I saw the small cottage from the brochure.

I could not help but gasp at the sight of a man standing in the middle of the road as we pulled up. Maya looked over at me and knew what was running through my mind.

"It is all right, that is Max. He is a friend of mine. I called him while you were paying for your items. I have a gift for you, and that is why he is here," Maya said with a smile that went on forever.

Maya could see that I was starting to relax, and the look on my face made Maya laugh.

"I asked him to give you the best alarm system to protect your home and property so you will feel more secure living alone. I hope you do not mind," Maya said as she exited the car and unlocked the back doors to start unloading my things.

As I watched Maya, I felt a sense of happiness wash over me; I had not felt this way in a long time. Then, turning, I opened the door, got out, and made my way towards the cottage door as I fumbled for the keys the previous owner had sent to my post office box. When I finally found them, I opened the door; I could feel the strength I had had so long waiting to return to me.

I had been waiting so long for my dream house that I could not believe it had finally come true. Finally, I was standing in the doorway to what I could see was the most beautiful place this world could have bestowed upon me. It was as if I had built it myself.

The loft faces the ocean so the morning's sun can shine gracefully, bringing forth the start of a new day with everything in the right place.

I stood there, taking in all the beauty of my new home. I almost forgot about the two people standing and watching me with smiles that I could never describe, even if I had tried. It was as if they were watching a child at Christmas getting all she had ever wanted.

"Well... let us get this car unloaded," Max said as he turned on his heels and headed for the car.

"Indeed," Maya said as she followed Max to the car.

"It looks like this is going to take all day to unload and set up," Maya continued as I turned to see her running to help with all I had bought.

She looked like a woman that had just found the greatest treasure in the world.

We unloaded the car in silence; this gave me time to relish the excitement of my new start. As I pulled on one of the last bags, I could hear the rumbling in my stomach growing louder, and I knew that the others could also and may also be hungry.

"I will install Maya's gift in the morning since we have a lot of work to do before I can get my job done," Max said.

"If it is all right with you two beautiful ladies, I will stay and help with all you have embarked upon," Max said, looking at us with the hope that it was all right for him to stay.

"It is fine by me," Maya said as she looked toward me, hoping I would agree.

"That would be great if you are sure it will not take you away from your work," I said gratefully.

I finished unloading the car and headed for the kitchen with the last bag; as I looked around the kitchen, I could see that I could cook anything my heart desired here. But it needed to be cleaned before I could fix our evening meal.

I was rushing to find my bag of cleaning supplies. I started hurrying around, cleaning the counters and the rest of the area to cook an excellent dinner for my newfound friends. I placed the dishes I had just bought in the dishwasher, and when I had them filled and running,

I returned to cleaning the cabinets, so I would have a place to store them when they finished. Finally, I unloaded the dishwasher with a clear and clean center island bar and put the new dishes in the proper places.

The window above the sink could hold the herbs I had obtained that morning. I set my things in place for preparing the evening meal. Standing at the stove in the center of the island bar, I could not help but smile. My aquatints were enjoying their glasses of wine and painting the bottom area with the sandy cream paint I had chosen for the outside.

However, it looked better here, so I did not say anything and went on to prepare the evening meal. I had decided to cook chicken parmesan, mashed potatoes, and green beans with freshly baked rolls to complete the meal. In addition, I would serve the black forest cake I had picked up from the bakery that morning for dessert.

Maya and Max moved the rest of the furniture outside onto the back deck as I cooked so they did not get any paint on it.

Then, with the meal started and my company busy, I returned to cleaning what was left of the kitchen so they would have a nice place to eat.

I decided to paint the walls in the kitchen area in the morning; I could see that the cabinets only needed to be washed and the wood treated to bring them back to life. So, I filled the sink with the cleaner that I felt would be the best to get my cabinets back to life; as I cleaned, I kept a close eye on the meal I was preparing for my guests.

Maya and Max had the living room area painted and moved into the space I had decided would make a great place for painting, sitting, and reading.

I watched as their noses sniffed the enticing aroma of the cooked meal.

I had been so busy cooking and cleaning the kitchen that I had not seen them approach me with the barstools.

When she saw the fabric beside the island bar, Maya wiped them down the stools and set them in place. Maya could not believe her eyes; she started to giggle.

"I would have never considered getting the material to update the furnishings." She said.

"We can reupholster these after dinner, Milly," Maya said as I sat on the bar stool beside Max.

"Oh, Maya, that can wait till tomorrow. Let us enjoy dinner and maybe get some more painting and cleaning done before we get too tired to do it," I said.

I served a healthy beef stew and set it down before two hungry-looking people. We ate and discussed everything I wanted to see done in my new home.

Max told me about the new alarm system he would put in while we reupholstered the barstools.

I told them I would like to buy a new living room set in the morning; however, I was curious if they would deliver it the same day or what I would do with the old stuff there.

Max said he could store it for me in his shed until I could figure out what I wanted to do with it.

I was surprised at the kindness I was being shown, and I knew my heart was filled with love for these two people helping me; they did not ask for anything in return.

All I could think about now was why these two had been so kind to me. Are all the people on this island this kind?

After dinner, we went out and sat on the back deck and watched the water. At the same time, we drank our wine and talked about how Maya and I would ask the Blaines about selling their Coffee Shop.

Max thought he had heard that Mr. Baines had passed away three weeks ago and Mrs. Baines had closed the store.

He said he would check it out when they were done getting me set up.

Max also told me that the people on the island were all like family and helped out anyone man who came to make the land their home.

He was hoping that this would put my mind at ease. However, he sensed that I had come from a hard life and was not used to people being kind or willing to help newcomers.

I got to my feet and headed back into the kitchen to set it in order. Then, with the sink still full of my cleaning solution, I started wiping down all the counters and placing liners and the finished ones. I then unboxed the dishes I had bought and put them in what I felt was the right place for them.

The cups, glasses, saucers, and plates were placed in the cabinet by the sink; the pots and pans hung over the island bar. Finally, the food went into the remaining cabinets. I still had many empty, so I made a list of the things I had not picked up.

I cleaned the drawers and put the utensils in the appropriate place. The eating utensils on the top and the ones I would cook with under them; the knives had their holder, so I set them on the counter where I had placed my cutting board.

Then I made a pot of coffee. I put three cups on the counter. I waited until the coffee maker was done brewing before I made my way to the others to start helping them paint the remaining downstairs.

When we had it all done, Maya headed up to the loft.

"What color do you want up here, Milly?" Maya yelled down.

"It all will be the same, Maya. The outside gets the sand cream, and the trim will be deep earth brown; however, we can do that in the morning," I yelled back up to Maya.

~ Making it My Own ~

"YEAH, LASS, IT IS GETTING late, and I need to be getting home," Max yelled to Maya.

"Wait, Max... Please do not leave two women here alone without any protection," Maya called down as she made her way to the main floor.

"Oh, Maya, you are not going to try and talk me into staying the night, are you?" Max said that as he winked at me, I knew that Maya would do just that.

"She always does this when she wants to spend time with me," Max whispered.

"Well, it is late, Max. You are more than welcome to stay with Maya in the loft. I can make the bed for you if you like," I said.

I turned to see Maya had already started back up the stairs with one of the new bedding sets.

"All right, I will stay as long as you stay in bed, and Maya and I will sleep here on the floor or the pullout. It would be best if you did not give up your comfort for us. Anyways this is your first night in your new home. So, you should at least sleep comfortably," Max said.

"Please take the bed; I can sleep on the couch and still be comfortable. You are all doing me the honor of staying with me and helping me get settled in," I said.

"No, Lass, Maya, and I will sleep on the pullout. So, you get some good rest in your loft bed. It will keep me down here to keep the two of you safe. If we were in the loft and someone broke in, you would be the first one they *would encounter. So, get ready for bed, and Maya and I will guard down here." Max informed us.*

As I got ready for bed, I could hear Maya and Max whispering while they made up the hid away bed.

"How could you think about sleeping in that woman's bed, Maya?" Max growled at her.

"I am sorry, Max, I was not thinking at all. I was excited you agreed to protect my new friend." Maya said with a tear-filled voice.

"Come now, Lass, do not cry. It breaks my heart when you do. Come now, Lass, let us sleep; we have a lot to do in the morning, and I guess we will need a few more hands to take out the old furniture and help get the new." Max said.

"Okay, Max, let us get some sleep. I know things will be brighter in the morning, and you will have the place wired for security, and then you can take us to have a great lobster dinner to celebrate our new friend." Maya said as she crawled into bed, and Max slid beside her.

I did not sleep well that night and could not quit feeling like my house was not mine; however, I knew it would be with time.

I slowly and quietly slid out of bed and went down the stairs to find Max at the stove cooking our morning meal. I saw that Maya was still fast asleep on what looked to be the most uncomfortable mattress.

"Good morning, Max; how did you sleep?" I quietly inquired.

"As well as could be on an old mattress, Lass," Max told me as he set a plate of the most amazing-smelling waffles on the table before me.

I just sat there watching him as he made himself at home in my kitchen. I could not believe a man as big as he was; could move so gracefully around a tiny area and not miss a step in his actions.

A strange sound had me pulling my gaze from Max to look over at the sofa to see Maya starting to wake. The look on her face was like she had smelled the most amazing thing in the world.

Max had a giant smile on his face as he walked over and put a cup of cinnamon coffee under her nose. So, Maya has a thing for cinnamon that Max has adapted to his morning coffee routine just for her.

I watched as Maya sniffed the air, slowly opened her sizeable brown eye, and smiled at Max. I could not help but see the love they both showed one another and envied them.

"Awe, Lassie, you need to rise and shine, darling. You know we have work to do, and then we need to go and talk to Mr. and Mrs. Blaines about selling their shop. We will need to see if they will take monthly payments for it, but I do not see why they would not." Max stated.

I sat at the island bar drinking a fantastic cup of coffee Max had set before me and listened to him try and sweet talk Maya out of the couch's most uncomfortable-looking bed. I knew that piece of furniture would be the first thing to go.

While I listened to him and Maya whisper, I thought about all the articles leaving this wonderful place. I could not help but feel a little sorry for the men taking the heavy pieces out of it.

This morning will be hectic, and the list in my mind keeps growing more and more extensive by the hour. Money seems to be dwindling by the wayside, with each object going on the list.

I will keep the essentials, like the most beautiful bookcases, end tables, coffee tables, kitchen tables, and handmade chairs.

I also know that I still can never let my guard down. He is out there, and he will find me, but for now, I will try to make a new life here in this place I can call home and be somewhat free of the pain Lawrence had put me threw. The nightmares I live when I close my eyes.

I need to find a way to free myself from the suffering I endured to get to this place of sanctuary.

"Milly? Are you okay?" Maya asked while Max looked on with concern I could see in his eyes.

"Huh? Oh, sorry, yes, I am fine. I was thinking about what needs to be done before inquiring about the Coffee Shop, Book Store that will become

my heavenly job." I informed them of half-truths, not what was scaring me out of what little wits I had left.

"Let us have breakfast before we finish the painting and remove the furniture from the living area. Well, all but the bookcases and end tables and coffee table. The mattress in the loft needs to be replaced with something a little softer, the office nook needs a new chair, and the desk needs to be sanded down and refinished. The bathroom needs new towels and such put away. And plunger and toilet bowl brush, and it all should be done by the end of today, and maybe tomorrow we can call upon your friends about the Coffee/Book shop?" Milly inquired f the couple standing in front of her.

"If you do not mind helping me clean this place out?" Milly shyly probed.

"Nah, Lass, we do not mind at all. I have already called and have two strapping young lads on the way over to help cart off the items you do not wish to keep. I hope ya do not mind me calling them in?" Max solicited.

"No, I do not mind. I hope the young men are strong enough to carry out that big sofa and the bed upstairs. The only things I want to keep are the handmade wooden furniture. The rest can go. Along with that big table in the dining area, I want to turn it into an office area. And the office area into a nook for books with tall bookshelves and comfortable seats." Milly informed her company.

"That sounds like a grand plan, Miss Milly," Maya told her new friend.

"We can have the furniture out of your way in a couple hours, but what are you going to replace it with, Lass" Max inquired.

Milly did not know what she wanted to replace the old one with but knew it had to be made of logs and comfortable. She no longer wanted a hideaway bed or light things that could be easily thrown.

She wants to feel safe in her own home. Looking around, she saw that the stuff she had bought the night before was all dark brown and deep greens; everything almost looked black.

It seemed that bright colors were not to her taste any longer.

"I would like to have log furniture with fluffy cushions. This is a log home, and I feel it would be beautiful with all log furniture and bookcases that go from the ceiling to the floor," Milly told her companions.

"Well, then, let us get to it after breakfast. That is when the boys will be here, and we can get the rest of the place cleaned up and ready for the new furniture. I will have the boys follow us in the flatbed to get your new stuff and bring it back here safe and sound." Max stated.

Everyone agreed that would be a grand idea and ate what Max had made that morning for the fuel their bodies would need for the hard work ahead of them.

By the time Max' friend arrived, the morning meal was done, and we girls were finishing up the last of the painting. Max brought them in to introduce them to Maya and me; however, Naya already knew them. The six-foot-five blond, goatee, very muscular bronze-skinned one is Max's half-brother Kieran.

The tawny-haired bearded one is almost seven feet and has a bodybuilder physique with a deep brown skin tone, is their cousin Sean walked through my front door and made me feel way too small and fragile.

I knew I had nothing to fear, but their size was intimidating, and their looks were too perfect. They got to work on removing the furniture that Max told them I wanted to get rid of to the flatbed truck.

When Maya and I were done painting, it was time to go to the furniture store Max had suggested, which happened to be Sean's.

Maya, Max, and I got into Max's truck, and the other two climbed into the flatbed. We made our way to Sean's store to get the furniture; I wanted to replace the items I had taken away.

I saw the most beautiful end tables in the display window as we arrived and knew I had to have them. They were all wooden logs with the cutest little draws and crystal nobs. The top looked to have been hand polished to shine like glass.

I could not wait to see what his store had to provide, so I jumped out of the truck before it completely stopped. I knew I would be in trouble for doing so, but I did not care at that point. I just had to be in that store, and it had to be now.

Entering the store, I saw the sofa I wanted and the perfect coffee table, and there was the most fantastic desk so I could write novels on the new laptop I had bought the day before.

The canopy four-poster bed with the dark forest green drapes was to die for. Then the night tables sitting next to the sleigh bed would excellently match the bed, and bookcases on the far wall were just what I needed, and my house would be set. I ran to all the artifacts I saw and came across two barstools that had been started but not finished yet, and I was sad that I would not be able to obtain those until they were done.

Running back to Max and Maya, I started pointing out everything I wanted. Max could not help but laugh at my exuberance and seemed to forget my blunder about jumping from the truck before it had stopped or Maya informed him about me being an abused person.

By the time I left, I had spent over twenty-five thousand dollars. It seemed to make Sean's smile was more prominent with everything I pointed out to furnish my cabin in the woods.

"Are you going to be able to take all this to the cabin?" I inquired of Sean.

"Eye Lassie, We will have it at your place and put it in place without trouble; however, lass, you have not gotten any lights to sit upon this nice furniture," Sean said smugly.

He was right; I had not found any that would fit the style I was aiming for. They would have to be ceramic, and he had nothing here that fit my idea of what would go with everything I had acquired.

"Milly lass, if you follow me next door, you might find what you are looking for there," Kieran stated, unsure of himself.

Looking to Maya and Max to see if they heard, I got a nod and watched as they came toward me. I followed Kieran out the door and saw the store he was leading to me; what a ceramic shop with great-looking pieces of nick-nacks that would go wonderfully in the cabin.

The knee-high family of grey wolves would look great by the river stone fireplace. The foot-high black worg book ends would fit nicely in the new bookcase to hold my books. The Indian-designed umbrella stand would be great to put flowers in.

As I shopped, I saw that Maya and Max looked at items. From my peripheral vision, I saw that they watched each piece I pointed to for Kieran to set aside for me, saw them get other things, and placed them with mine. I did not know what they were doing or why they got something they thought I might like, but I left them to it. Maybe they were shopping for his home while I shopped for mine.

When I was done shopping and Maya and Max purchased their items and mine, Kieran told us he would use his van to deliver them today while Sean got Bruse to help him with the furniture.

We had just arrived when Sean, Bruse, and Kieran pulled up ten minutes later with all the treasures I had procured that day.

I opened the double doors so it would be easier for them to bring in the pieces and place them where I wanted them. As I directed, I saw that Maya and Max were bringing in the item we had gotten from the ceramic shop and started to unwrap them all. I saw the things I had bought and the ones they had acquired and watched as they began to place them.

By the time everything was put in place, the bed had been made, it was time for dinner; when I went to the kitchen, I saw that Kieran and Max were at the store already cooking, and the smell of beef stew permeated the air. The small table I kept had enough room for all six of us to comfortably sit and converse.

"Come on, Lass, sit while we will serve the food and wine, I will get the others, and then we can say grace when all are seated," Max said as he served up the stew and Kieran poured the wine.

I watched as Kieran called all to dinner, and the hoards of people rushed to the table.

"Kieran, please, it is your turn to say grace," Max informed his brother.

"Our heavenly father bless this mean we are about to receive, bless the good coming and good fortune we received this day. May you guide us in your holy way and keep us from hard, amen," Kieran imparted.

We talked about going to Mr. And Mrs. Baines's shop in the morning since the cabin was done and I needed to make a living at something I would enjoy; their store was already set up for what I was looking for the only thing I would need to do was restock it with updated supply.

When all were done eating and the dishes washed, they headed for the door.

"We will return in the morning around six am to take you to see the Baines and set you up to open your new adventure in this life you have set before you, Lass," Max divulged.

~ Opening the New Shop~

AFTER CHECKING THE doors server times, I ultimately made my way to the loft. I set the alarm for five am to be up, have breakfast, then climbed into bed. I had a hard time sleeping that night. I had not been alone in so long that it took me several hours to finally feel safe enough to fall asleep.

It did not seem as if I had been asleep for long when I heard the alarm going off and had to get out of bed to turn it off. If I had set it close to the bed, I would not have gotten up, so placing it on the dresser to force me to get up was the best yet terrible idea.

Getting up, I turned off the alarm,d gathered the clothing I wanted to wear that day, and made my way down to the bathroom to get showered and brush my teeth. On my way to the shower, I stopped, turned on the coffee maker, and started the shower setting it to very hot to cleanse off the muck from the previous days.

When I stepped out of the shower, I heard Maya yelling at the door to be let in from the cold. Laughing at her plight, I got dressed and ran to the front door to let her and Max in; I saw him rolling his eyes at Maya's antics.

"Come on, Lass, let us get in and get you warmed up with a cup of coffee so you are not freezing your cute little tush off," Max told Maya as they slid past me and headed towards the kitchen, where the coffee had already started.

I watched as Maya got down three large cups and filled them all with coffee; she turned and set one in front of Max and then one to the side for me. She seemed to be making herself at home, and I did not seem to mind, which seemed strange.

"Okay, on today's agenda, we are going to see Mr. and Mrs. Baines, then head to the coffee/book shop. We will see what needs to be taken care of there. Then if you want, I can call the boys again to have them available to remove whatever you do not want there. Then we can set it up, however you like after that," Max enlightened me.

"Let us see if I can get the shop before we call anyone. Then if we need to, we will get Sean and Kieran to come by with the flatbed to take things away. However, I will need to see that place before making any plans," I divulged to them.

"Alright, Lass, we will play it by ear," Max stated, heading for the sink to put his cup away and then turning for the door to start the day.

I had a feeling this day would be either short or very long. Yet it was something I was looking forward to. I could wait to meet the couple about the store and find out if they would allow me to purchase it.

Placing my cup next to Max's, I headed for the door and heard Maya moan about not finishing her coffee.

"Max, you owe me a nice hot coffee since you are in such a mood," Maya yelled out the door at him.

"Anything you say, Lass," Max yelled back.

After we all climbed into Max's truck, we headed in the southern direction, away from the small town and deeper into the mountains.

Feeling slightly discomfort, Maya reached over and took my hand, reassuring me that all was well and not to worry so much.

After that small gesture, I relaxed and watched the trees fly past the window. I had not realized I had fallen asleep until Maya woke me a short time later while laughing at Max.

"Huh? What is so funny, Maya?" I inquired.

"You kind of snort when you sleep," Maya informed me, and I saw Max trying his hardest not to laugh.

All I could do was huff at Max, and head for the front porch of what I hoped was the Baines house. It is a cute little homestead with a larger-than-life barn towering over the tiny house.

"Marget, Charles, are you home?" Max hollered up the driveway.

"Max, you stop the bellowing and come in. You also bring that sweet Maya and whoever else you have out there. You know better than to holler at my door, boy," Marget yelled from somewhere inside.

I could not help laughing at the look on Max's face and how pink it was turning. All Maya did was roll her eyes and open the door for us to enter the tiny home of the Baines.

"Come on back; we are in the kitchen having our morning meal. You all want some coffee or tea?" Charles called out as we made our way toward the voice.

"Coffee, please, Mrs. Marget," Maya called back.

I thought it would be rude to yell out for a drink when I did not know the people. I saw Maya roll her eyes at me and yell, "Make that three, Mrs. Marget,"

When we finally reached the kitchen, I saw that the place was more extensive than it looked.

After we all took our seats at the round table that appeared to be one Sean had made, Max wasted no time enquiring about their shop and how I was looking to buy the place unseen. However, Marget would not let me purchase the place site unseen.

"We will head over there after breakfast," Charles avowed.

We talked about how I had bought the Winter's cabin. And refurnished, it will a lot of Sean's pieces and how I wanted to put in a garden in the spring and what I would need to do to get the plants to grow since the ground in that part of the world was more rocky than the soil. I wanted a business that would let me be free to be myself. How I wanted in my spare time to write my own novels.

The Baines's listened to what I would like to do and did their hums and grunts in between while they ate. When they were finished, Mrs. Baines did the dishes saying never leave what can be done now for later, for the bugs will come a calling if ya do. Making me think of the three cups unattended in my own sink.

After that, we made our way out to the truck while the Baines got into a small Sudan; we pulled out of the drive and followed them into town.

Now the town is small, making you think of one of those Western-themed places where you would take your children to learn about the past.

It has a restaurant, a hotel, and a small flower shop with Seans and Kieran's ceramic and woodworking shop. They even have a blacksmith; only the gods and goddesses know what is made in that place.

The coffee/bookstore sits at the end of the main street and looks like it came out of a medieval romance novel on the outside.

We parked in front of the shop and made our way to the door while Mr. Baines helped his wife from their car and up the curb to the door.

While Mr. Baines unlocked the door, Mrs. Baines told me about the store and how it did not make that much money but was her place to escape the house.

She talked about how she loved to sit and drink coffee while reading her favorite books or watching people going about their day.

When we finally entered the building and saw what was there, I knew I had to make the place come to life again and bring in a lot more than was there.

It needed a place where people could sit and drink coffee after buying their books or other little trinkets, like book markers and little stuffies for the children accompanying their parents.

The bookshelves would have to be replaced with the ones I had bought at Sean's place, and little bens for stuffies and maybe a play area for the kids so their parents could get a small break away.

I had a lot of ideas running through my head when I finally heard Mrs. Baines talking to me.

"I am sorry I was lost in thought. Can you please repeat yourself?" I gently asked.

"That is alright, child. I was just wondering if you were okay." Mrs. Baines inquired of me.

"Oh yes, I am fine. I saw all the ways I could make this place my home away from home. I was also thinking about how it would be a great place to give mothers a break from their children with a play area for them. And a comfortable nook so the mothers could still see their kids and be able to read and drink their beverages. How Sean's bookshelves would be wonderful in here and all the new material adorning them. I saw a ben for the kids to get a stuffy to play with; I am sorry, my mind is reeling with all kinds of possibilities," I informed her.

"Then we better get to the negotiations, so you can make your dreams come true, girlie," Mr. Baines stated and sat down at the only table.

Sitting beside him while Mrs. Baines took Maya and Max on a small tour.

"Mr. Baines, I have ninety-four thousand dollars left of the money I brought. I hope you will be kind enough to let me buy your store for forty thousand if that seems fair," I informed him.

"Now, girlie, that is way more than a fair price for this rundown shop, I heard you telling the misses about all you want to do to this place, something she told me we should have done in the beginning, but I was hearing none of it so let us say you give me the forty k and we will help you clean this place up and be your first customers when you get your merchandise in hows that sound to you?" Mr. Baines questioned.

Not being able to say anything, I just rapidly nodded my head and hugged the old man. He patted my back and shushed me, knowing I had agreed with the conditions of our agreement.

"Marget, we are headed to the bank to sign the papers to this place over to this young lady. You coming with me, or do you want to wait here?" Mr. Baines asked his wife.

"You go on, Charles, me and these two will wait here for the other boys to show up and start cleaning up this place. Milly girl, what color do you want this place painted," Mrs. Baines queried.

"I was thinking a light sandy color for all the walls and Sean's bookshelves for the far right wall so that it goes from ceiling to floor and wall to wall, if that is okay?" I questioned the woman.

"Girlie, this is going to be your place, and you will need that Sean boy to make you a play area for kids you see coming with those worn-out mothers to have a break from. Now you get on out of here and sign them there papers. We will get the paint you want and the bookshelves from Sean's place and more help to get this place up and running in the next few days," Marget told them all.

Milly and Charles made their way to the bank, and Max and Maya went to get Sean, Keiran, and the bookcases.

When Milly and Charles entered the bank, the bank manager was on his way to greet them and lead them to his office; Max had called ahead to let him know what was going on and make things run smoothly.

"Good morning, Charles and Lass. I have the documents ready to be filled out and the transaction of money transfer to your account Mr. Baines. I am Stephen, by the way; you let me know if you need anything," He told us and left the room.

"Well, Lass, let us get this done and the title to the building signed over to you," Mr. Baines instructed me.

"Mr. Baines, sir, I can pay you, but it will have to come off this card since I do not have an account here. If that is alright with you. You can check it and see that all the money is on it; if you would like, I can give you the pin number or the banker and take it off with my information. It is up to you, sir," I informed him of the problem of the money not being in an account.

"Let me see that card, Lassie," Charles asked. He took the card and saw it was prepaid, eyeing me dubiously.

"Please do not ask, sir; I wish not to relive the time before I came here," I pleaded with him.

"Not to worry, girlie, I can see that it does not have your name on it, so this will be good; no need to bother the banker," Mr. Baines informed me with a wink.

Once all the paperwork where signed and notarized, the banker inquired about the payment for the transaction. Mr. Baines then told him to mind his own and leave the money dealing to us.

We then returned to the shop and saw more than six people painting the walls and the ceiling the same color, making the place look more welcoming. I saw Sean in the far left corner building a play area. It had a small sandbox and a mini jungle gym with a swing; the whole thing resembled a castle.

I saw that the right wall where I wanted the bookcase was by the window, and the children's area would have been better there.

"Yum, Sean? I wondered how hard it would be to move the bookcases and the children's area? I cautiously asked.

I saw Sean and Kieran look at the bookcases and then the play area and knew they saw what I wanted; with a smile and a tilt of his head to the other two men, they moved everything in mere minutes. I knew I was right when I had them move it all and knew the others could see what I had done to entice the parents to come into the shop. It is a sneaky but good business maneuver.

I gave Marget the list of books, how many to buy, and a twenty thousand dollar card to purchase everything I would need. I watched as she went to the computer in the back office and started acquiring all the items I wanted for this store. The coffee machine was brand new and had not been used much.

Everything I wanted was being bought or made, and I paid Sean and Keiran for all the work and items they had made. I had shelves with vases filled with flowers and pottery candy dishes with small bracelets or wrapped candy.

We spent three days getting the shop set up to open next week. I was so happy when I saw the finished shop and was ready to get to work selling all the items.

It happened then that dreadful feeling as though something grave was about to happen. With that feeling of doom weighing me down, I went to the office and wrote my will and testament. I left everything to Maya and Max. They were co-owners of the Coffee Shop.

When I was done, I took the paperwork to the bank. I had Stephen notarize it so that there was no way the husband could claim anything and sign over the deed to the shop and house to them simultaneously. The bank manager looked at me as though I had lost my mind after only having the place for a week; however, he did not ask any questions.

I will have to inform Max and Maya of
what I have done and hope they will not
ask questions.

~Danger Comes~

MAYA DROVE ME HOME that night, yet I could not bring myself to tell her she was now the owner of my house and the Coffee Shop.

We made plans to redo the apartment above the shop for a renter, someone who was a little down on their luck, or a college student who wanted to work at the Coffee Shop for extra money. However, we decided to wait on that for now. I was running low on funds and wanted to ensure I had enough to pay for the employees I would need when the time came.

When we pulled into the driveway, Maya looked concerned. "What is wrong, Milly?" she finally questioned.

"There is nothing wrong, Maya. I am excited and tired and desperately need a good night's sleep; I also worry no one will come to the store's opening. Do you think we will get customers?" I probed her.

"Awe, don't worry, little sister, we will have a house full. Sean and Keirn have been putting out fliers and spreading the word about your shop. Max called his sisters and cousins. So we will be pretty busy next week. This will also give us time to ensure everything is in place and ready to greet everyone walking through the door." Maya articulated me with a giant smile on her face.

"Okay, I will try not to worry about not having people coming to the store and getting a good night's sleep," I divulged to her.

Getting out of the car, I made my way toward my cabin, which was mine for now; I heard Maya drive away, and I knew then how she would find me in a week before the store was to be opened.

Sure enough, when I opened the door, he sat in the dark, watching me approach, and Maya leave. I knew I could not make a sound, or the beating I knew was coming would be so much worse than the ones he had given me in that basement in Colorado.

He did not move until he saw that Maya's car was long gone, and then he did not move for another hour. He just sat there. I made my way into the kitchen and found that all my sharp instruments were gone, so I made myself a cup of coffee and at the small table to drink it. I made sure to face him.

I wanted to see him coming this time. I wanted to be ready for his first lunge. Then it came, and I was not prepared for it.

His fist struck me in the side of the head, knocking me to the floor, and without warning, he was on top of me, holding my arms pinned to the ground.

With every blow, I knew I was about to die. Letting my body go lax, I meet the darkness I know was inevitable. When I came around, I was still on the kitchen floor, and My husband Lawrence was again sitting on the living room sofa.

"You know, wife, you owe me two hundred and forty-two thousand dollars, and before I release you from this world, you will be giving me my money," Lawrence informed me. I knew then I would not be dying soon, and the punishment will get worse for me escaping him.

I slept in the kitchen that night while he rested on the sofa. The following day I could not open my eyes because they were swollen shut. He told me to make him breakfast, but I could not see to do so, and he again beat me for not complying with his order, telling me he owned me and I had better remember that.

Again I lost consciousness and did not wake until two days later; he told me I would pay and proceeded to break my arm. I remember letting out a scream that hurt my throat.

The next time I came to was three hours later, and he started again asking where his money was, and I kept silent. When he asked me any question, I kept quiet.

I knew he would never find the card or the will leaving everything to my friend and her love. That day at the bank, I opened a safety deposit box leaving instructions that the contents be given to Maya if I was found dead.

I had also pinned a note to her giving her my real name and who had killed me so the police would find him.

When I came through the fifth time, I was held by Maya crying, saying she should have come sooner. Both my arms had been broken in three places, and my calves had been harmed.

I could not move; nevertheless, I could hear someone being beaten. Sean was also screaming at Max to stop, or he was going to kill him. It seemed Sean was a little upset, as though Max was not letting him have a turn at the man.

The next thing I knew and could feel was the bumping of wheels and the turning of helicopter blades in the distance.

Someone was moving me across the floor, and the ribs my husband had broken made it painful to breathe. I tried to tell the person moving me, but no words would come out due to the fact my jaw was broken.

"Shhh, sweetheart, you are okay; we will take you to the hospital and get you well. Then we will open that beautiful shop of yours," Sean said. Still, the thing I was lying on, I could feel my rib being pushed into my right lunge, and I knew I would not make it to the hospital even by helicopter.

Nonetheless, I could not tell anyone what was happening with a broken jaw and difficulty breathing.

I was right; I did not make it to the hospital before I died the first time. They had brought me back once and realized I had seven broken ribs, and one had punctured my right lung when they tried CPR on me.

I felt the helicopter land and let out a quiet cry of pain. That is when they realized my jaw had been broken. After that, I felt nothing and saw nothing.

I heard the doctor say they would have to put me in an induced coma that I might never wake up from, but it was something they needed to do to keep me alive.

When I woke, I saw Maya and Max sleeping in the chairs beside me. That is when I knew I had survived the worse beating of my short life.

My arms and legs were in casts, and my ribs were hurting. Nonetheless, I could breathe; I felt something pulling my skin like it had been pried open.

I must have made a noise because Max was on his feet looking around, and the monitor was going nuts.

"Maya, Lass, Milly is awake and in pain. Go get the doctor," Max whispered yelled.

Max saw I was trying to talk, "Do not try to speak, Little one. Your jaw is broken, and so are your extremities. You will need help getting around, eating, drinking, and so forth. The doctor said you will be in a wheelchair for three months. Then you are going to need physical therapy for six after that to regain your strength. The man that beat you so severely died in jail two days ago. You have been in the hospital for the past month and a half. The doctors said you are healing well and can go home as long as someone is always with you," Max said, trying to give me all the information he could.

I was never left alone. Maya, Max, Kieran, and Sean ensured one of them was always with me. For the next six weeks, I laid in bed, unable to move or scratch the itchies in my casts, driving me nuts.

When Maya finally reached my bedside, she saw the tears in my eyes and turned to smack Sean upside the head.

"Can't you see she needs something? You are a buffoon. Milly are you in pain? Is something bothering you, and you need to fix it like right now?" Maya asked, and for the first time, I could say gitchy.

With a vast smile, Sean got to his feet and went to the other side of the bed to use a soft covers dole and my right arm. And then my right leg, while Maya did the same to my left side.

"Just so you know, little lady, I asked the doctor when you can go home, and he said today sometime, but he wants to check you over again before releasing you." Sean apprised Milly.

I could not help but smile and ensure they could all see it. I could not wait to get back to my cabin in the woods. I also wanted to go to the coffee shop and see how it was doing. I did not know if Maya or Max had opened the shop. I hoped they waited for me to open it.

The next few months were hard after they released me from the hospital, and I had difficulty sitting in a wheelchair. But I managed, and every day

Maya and Max took me to the shop after the grand opening to get me out of the cabin for a while. I got to drink iced coffee and watch the people as they made their way around the shop drinking their beverages or eating a scone and reading books.

Sean asked me one day if I would like to watch him make his furniture or go to Kieran's ceramic shop to watch him create his work, but all I wanted to do was sit in my little store and people-watch.

Every night I would go home and watch tv with Maya or Sean, whoever drew the short straw for that day.

Then the day came for the wires holding my jaw shut to come off and all the casts removed. The doctor said I might need help walking or physical therapy to move again, but I was hoping to be able to walk out of the building with a bit of support.

Three hours later, with Maya on my left side and Max behind me, I could move with a bit of frustration and walked out the front door. I knew I would have to ask Maya to help me to the bathroom still and up and down stairs, but I did it, and yet I still had to go to physical therapy to strengthen my arms and legs.

It took another six weeks before I was moving on my own freely. Nonetheless, I had put in the work, could walk with a slight limp, and still working on holding a spoon without dropping it.

I worked hard on getting back to being somewhat normal. I was able to go to work every day and help stock the shelves and make coffee.

On the day of my birthday, I realized my dreams did come true, and so can yours.

~ About the Author ~

WHEN ASKED IF I WRITE about myself, I must sit back and try not to laugh. However, since my characters carry my pen name, I was told that my readers think it is about me.

The truth is, I write under my character's name since she is the one who is writing the books. I am just her instrument of use. The one that allows her to write through me. Now you might think I am crazy, but I can assure you I am just as sane as everyone else. I do not want people to know my real name. Those who do already think I have lost my ever-loving mind.

My family seems to think I should write successful conclusions where the hero or heroine lives happily ever after. Yet that is not me. I want to write about good/evil, happiness/devastation. I want it where my readers cry when they are happy or sad with the characters. I want them to want to do murder when the lousy person is out to harm another. But, I want my readers to cheer when the character finally has a happy time, and things have gone their way.

That is who I am. The kind of writer I want to be. So yes, I hide behind my main character. I use her to keep me safe.

Don't miss out!

Visit the website below and you can sign up to receive emails whenever Athinia Tandino publishes a new book. There's no charge and no obligation.

https://books2read.com/r/B-A-UKOL-UGIBC

BOOKS 2 READ

Connecting independent readers to independent writers.

Did you love *The Coffee Shop, A New Beginning*? Then you should read *Arkadia, A Druid's Tale*[1] by Athinia Tandino!

[2]

As we made our way through the city to the center, where Belialz said would be the place to call for the Dark Lord, something inside me seemed to come alive.I ran to his side, and with my father's scimitar in hand, I saw Adonys come to stand at my side as we tried to help Belialz fight this demon. Yet, neither one of us was as strong as the Paladin who stood toe-to-toe with the monstrous beast.As Luna took me to the battle site, I watched as Belialz fell to the ground; afraid that the Dark Lord was still alive, I ran to Belialz's side, trying to heal his wounds just as Moonstar had shown me.When you are gone from this world, where am I supposed to turn to find the love that I still yearn for?" I waited for the answers to all I wanted and needed to know.It was not

---

1. https://books2read.com/u/mV8qvP

2. https://books2read.com/u/mV8qvP

by coincidence that Steve sent you to hear my story," Athinia said as she watched the sun coming up out of the sea and saw Belialz coming around the corner of the small cottage with Adonys and Luna at his side.You had torn a rift between our worlds, the night you and your friend thought you could use magic to bring you, true love." Belialz told me.I need the help from your world and mine to stop the new evil that reigns over our lands," Athinia said as she turned and watched as I admired the beauty of her world."Sophie, if you look, you will see that you have the gift to bring forth life to both our worlds at your feet," Athinia said.As I glanced down, I saw that as I walked in the World of Arkadia, the ground beneath my feet had started to spring to life with flowers growing around them with every step I took.You see, this is not where our tale ends, for it is said that when you opened the rift between our two worlds, the Dark Lord of the mist came to life and sought the one that is preventing him from gaining what his brother truly desired.

Also by Athinia Tandino

Arkadia A Druid's Tale
Arkadia, A Druid's Tale
Arkadia, The Dark Mist Legend

Standalone
One Fine Morning, In a Town All Its Own
A Dream All Her Own
The Forgotten One.
The Coffee Shop, A New Beginning

About the Author

I was born in Canon City, Colorado, to Irish/Scottish parents, grew up in Canon City and Texas, now living in Florida for the last eleven years. My first book, "Arkadia a Druid's Tale," was published on March 1st, 2010. I love to write since I was 14 years of age but never thought myself good enough. When I met a man that encouraged me to fulfill my dreams at the age of 32 and still encourages me to move forward with my new works of art. Now I have the sequel to Arkadia and two others published. I hope you all will enjoy them.

When I'm asked if I write about myself, I have to sit back and try not to laugh. I was told that since my characters carry my pen name that my readers think it is about me.

The truth is, I write under my characters' name since she is the one who is really writing the book. I'm just her instrument of use. The one that allows her to write through me. Now you might think I'm crazy, but I can assure you, I'm just as sane as everyone else. I don't want people to know my real name. Those who do already think I have lost my ever-loving mind.

My family seems to think I should write successful conclusions, where the hero or heroine lives happily ever after. Yet that is not me. I want to write about good/evil, happiness/devastation. I want it where my readers are crying with the characters when they are happy or sad. I want them to want to do murder when the bad guy is out to harm another. I want my readers to cheer when the characters finally have a happy time and things have gone their way.

That is who I am. The kind of writer I want to be. So yes I hide behind my main character. I use her to keep me safe.